W9-BVD-722

LUPE LOPEZ

ROCK STAR RULES!

To Eva Goins and Cindy Vela, who celebrate
the rock star in all of their students —eEC-T

To LuEllen Childers and the rock stars at
St. James School in Madison, Wisconsin —PZM

For Juana, rock star teacher. Forever Rocktober!
—JC

First edition 2022. Library of Congress Catalog Card Number pending. ISBN 978-1-5362-0954-9 (English edition).
ISBN 978-1-5362-2006-3 (Spanish edition). This book was typeset in Adobe Caslon. The illustrations were created digitally.
Candlewick Press, 99 Dover Street, Somerville, Massachusetts 02144. www.candlewick.com.
Printed in Shenzhen, Guangdong, China. 22 23 24 25 26 27 CCP 10 9 8 7 6 5 4 3 2 1

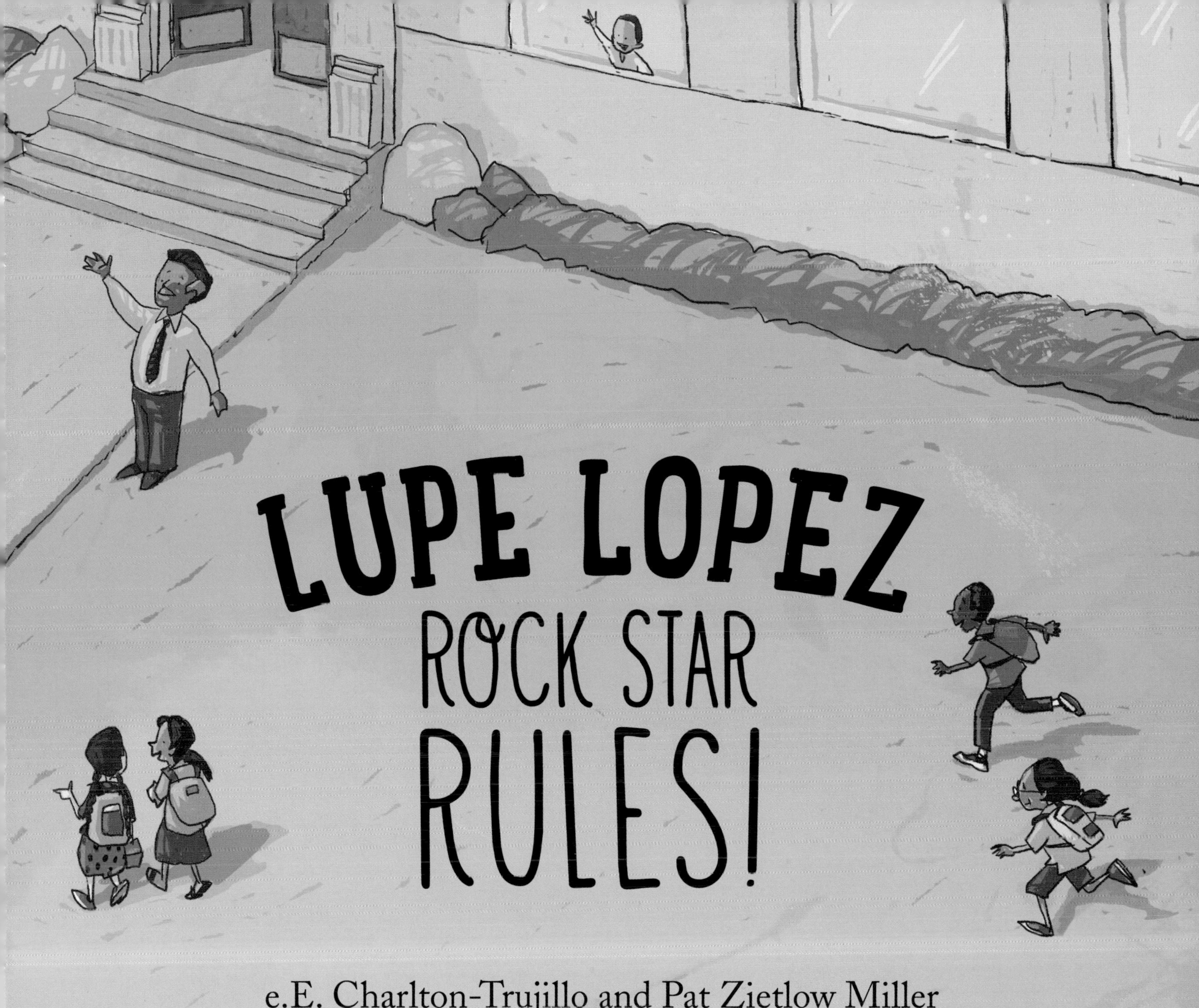

LUPE LOPEZ
ROCK STAR RULES!

e.E. Charlton-Trujillo and Pat Zietlow Miller

illustrated by Joe Cepeda

CANDLEWICK PRESS

Lupe Lopez had big plans for the first day of kindergarten.
She'd practiced drumming all summer.
And now, she was a real-life, Texas-size rock star.
As anyone could see.
She strutted through the doors of Hector P. Garcia
Elementary School . . .

Shiny sunglasses covering her eyes.
Her mother's classic lunch box bouncing at her side.
And two banged-up, taped-up
No. 2 pencils poking out of her pocket, ready to
drum at any time.

On any thing!

Desks.

Tables.

Chairs.

The Texas map on her classroom wall.

But then . . .

"Lupe Lopez!" said Ms. Quintanilla. "Take off those sunglasses."
Lupe grinned. And rolled out another solo on her classmates' desks.

"But I'm a rock star."

Lupe was the first kid to get in trouble on the first day of kindergarten. Which, to be honest, was kind of a big deal.

“We all have to follow rules,” Ms. Quintanilla said. “Especially in school.”

“Rock stars don’t follow rules,” Lupe said.

“Yes, they do,” said her teacher.

Then she listed three rules for being a school rock star:

2) USE YOUR INSIDE VOICE.

1) LISTEN TO YOUR TEACHER.
I did! Except once.
Rock and roll *is* my inside voice!
3) BE A FRIEND.
I'm a solo act.

"No more sunglasses. No more trouble," Ms. Quintanilla said. "Understand?"

Lupe tapped her fingertips against her hips, nodded her head, and said, "Cool . . ."

Which was a rock star way of saying she'd think about it.

But Lupe thought Ms. Quintanilla had her rules wrong.
Lupe knew rock stars:

1) Didn't listen to anyone.
2) Made lots of noise. *¡Rataplán!*
3) Had fans, not friends.

When Ms. Quintanilla asked Lupe to stop drumming and put her pencils away, Lupe followed her first rule—and didn't listen.

She kept making music instead.
She tried to do it quietly, but then . . .

Everyone laughed.
Except Ms. Quintanilla.

"You can have these back after school," she said.
Lupe sighed.
Now she had no sunglasses.
No drumsticks.
No lunch box.
And no star power.

During lunch, Lupe put on her
sunglasses and drummed a lunch-box beat.
A boy laughed.
"She thinks she's a rock star."
"I am a rock star," Lupe insisted.
She stood up. Gathered lunch trays.
Lined up milk cartons.
And followed her second rule
by making lots of noise.

“Rock stars listen to their teacher,” said Ms. Quintanilla. “Unless they want to lose their drumsticks.”

That was the one thing Lupe didn’t want.

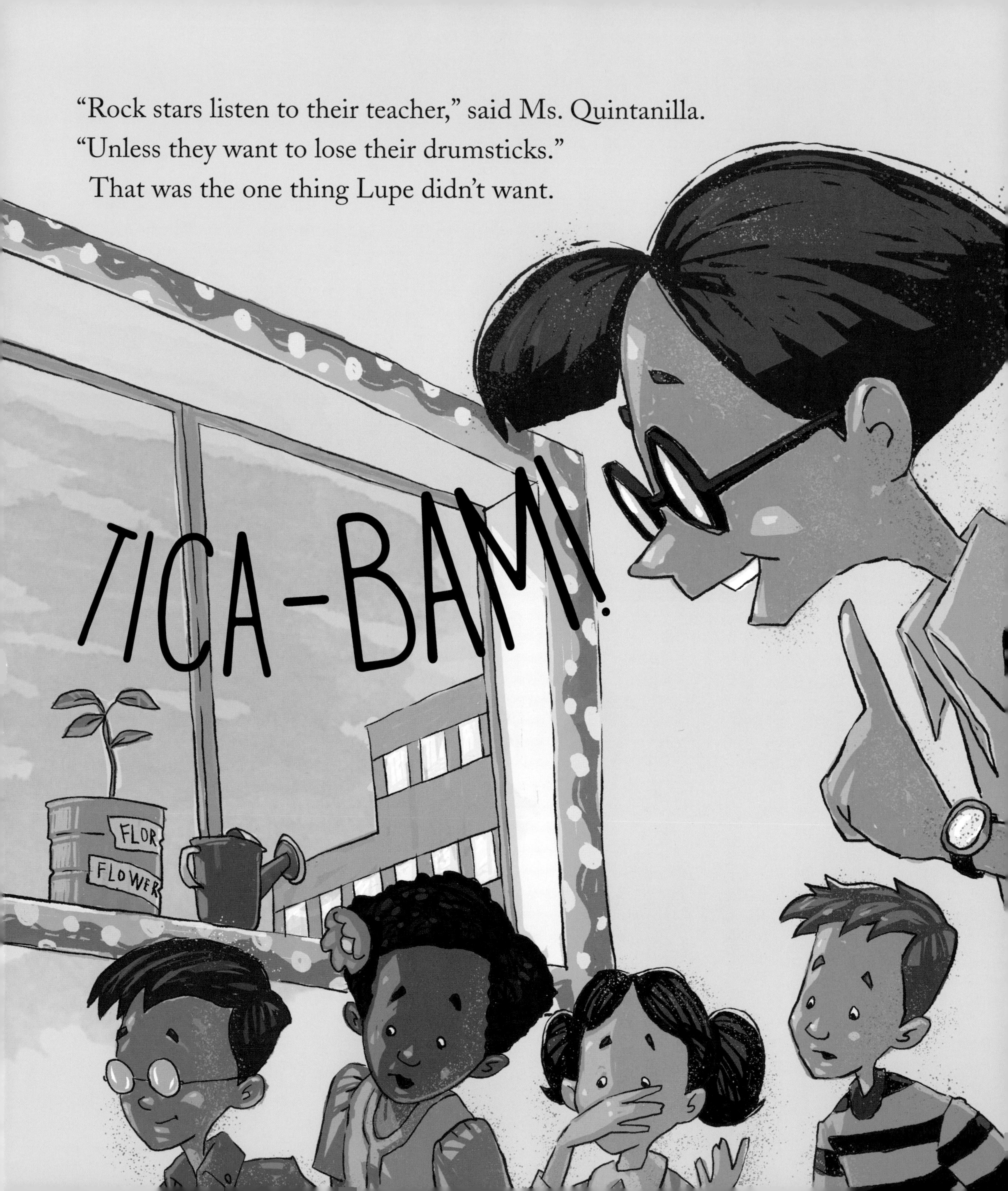

Ruby DeLeon and Ana Flores sat beside her.

"We love your drumming," said Ruby.

"You're kind of a big deal," said Ana.

"Really?" Lupe said. "You can be my first fans."

Ruby shook her head.

"We don't want to be fans. We want to start a band. I play guitar. And Ana sings."

At lunch, Lupe tapped a tiny beat with her fingers.
Barely loud enough to hear.
That's when . . .

It was the worst morning a kindergartner ever had at Hector P. Garcia Elementary.
As anyone could see.

SHE LISTENED POLITELY.

USED HER INSIDE VOICE.

TRIED TO BE A FRIEND.

AND DIDN'T DRUM ON ANYTHING AT ALL.

The next day, Lupe brought her lunch in a paper bag, put a plain pencil behind her ear, shut her sunglasses in her desk, and tried to follow Ms. Quintanilla's rules.

Maybe . . . her classmates hadn't heard her from
the top of the slide.
Maybe . . . they thought she meant tomorrow.
Or maybe . . . she wasn't a rock star after all.
Soy famosa, Lupe thought. *Yeah, right. I can't even get fans.*

After school, Lupe drummed with her fingers. She drummed with her toes. She even drummed with her elbows. The librarian had to shush her three times.

She waited and waited.
But no one came.

“Wanna roll with a rock star? Join my fan club!
Meet me after school in the library.”
Then she banged a beat with her feet and strutted to class.

She needed fans!
During recess, Lupe climbed the slide, struck a pose, and used her loudest rock-and-roll voice:

It was a Texas-size problem.
Until Lupe remembered her own third rule . . .

Lupe hadn't considered being in a band.
"Cool," she said. Which was a rock star way of saying she'd think about it.
"We can rock," insisted Ruby.
"And I can roll," said Lupe.
Maybe, thought Lupe, *friends are better than fans.*

The next morning, Lupe, Ruby, and Ana strutted through the doors of Hector P. Garcia Elementary.

Pencils and guitar picks waiting in their lunch boxes.
Sunglasses dangling from their shirts.
Ready to be famous—after school.
Because even rock stars follow the rules.

Sometimes.